SEASONS

BY:

JOIS DONKOR

Melanin Origins

Published by Melanin Origins

PO Box 122123; Arlington, TX 76012

First Edition

Library of Congress: 2023906023

Hardcover - 978-1-0880-9250-7

Soft Cover - 978-1-0880-9255-2

This book is dedicated to Mila & Julia Fenske and Olivia Olushoga, the little girls I had the opportunity to take care of when I moved to the US. I loved reading to you; it awakened my desire to write. I hope you're inspired and never let any SEASON stop you from achieving your goals. I love you.

THE TALK

NDELLA: Mama, Papa, I need to call George and let him know we will be moving to his country next month because of your new job.

MR. SAYE: Yes, why not. That is a good idea.

NDELLA: What questions can I ask about his country?

MRS. SAYE: Well, first you want to ask him how he is doing.

NDELLA: Of course, Ma. I was going to do that (rolls her eyes). I have good manners (they all laugh).

MR. SAYE: You can also ask about the weather and start from there.

NDELLA: Yup! You are right. Thank you both. I have the best parents.

NDELLA: Hi George, how are you?

GEORGE: I am good, thanks for asking. How about you?

NDELLA: I am good too, thank you. I bring you good news. My parents and I will be moving to your country next month. My dad got a new job there.

GEORGE: Oh wow, that is the best news I have heard today! I am so excited and cannot wait to see you! This will be our first-time meeting in person.

NDELLA: I am super excited too. You're right. It will be our first-time meeting. What is the weather like there right now?

GEORGE: Well, right now it is the fall season.

NDELLA: Hmm, can you tell me about it?

GEORGE: Well, you know there are different seasons in the world. Some countries have four seasons, so, here in America, we have Winter, Spring, Fall, and Summer.

NDELLA: Yes, of course! I know there are different seasons in the world. Did you know my country only has two seasons, Dry and Wet?

GEORGE: No! I never knew your country had two seasons.

NDELLA: The countries which have two seasons are close to the equator, so they are mostly hot and humid.

GEORGE: Ndella, have you experienced the four seasons?

NDELLA: No! But I knew your country had four seasons. I always see it on TV, on social media, and in books. I am shocked you have never heard of our two seasons before. This is about to be an interesting conversation.

GEORGE: Yup! I will tell you about mine even though I know you have an idea about them. I just want you to come prepared. And then you tell me about yours.

NDELLA: Sounds like a plan.

GEORGE: Okay, here we go. Let us start with winter. In Winter, it gets pretty cold, sometimes icy cold. Snow falls, but sometimes it is just freezing rain. With a lot of snow, you can build a snowman, go sledding or ice skating. People wear jackets, boots, scarves, gloves, and a hat to stay warm. The sun comes out a bit later and it gets dark earlier in the day as winter goes on.

NDELLA: Yes, I have seen that in the movies. I did not know the sun comes out late and it goes down early. How late and early are we talking about?

GEORGE: The sun comes out as late as 8 am and goes down as early as 2:30 pm sometimes. It is called the 'tilt of the earth,' meaning the sun is shining at a different latitude and angle.

NDELLA: Whoaaaaaa. Does that mean you go to bed early?

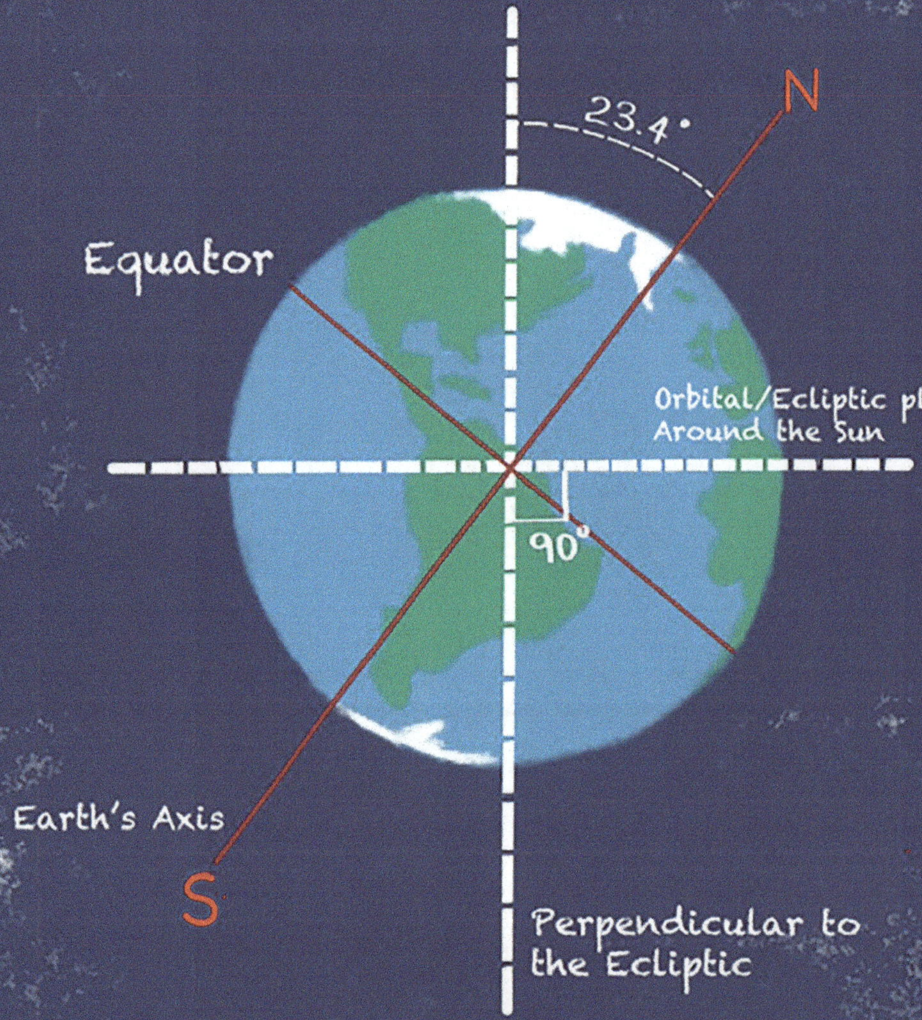

GEORGE: No, Ndella! I am mostly in school by that time. I still go to bed at my usual time, 8 pm on school days. You know how parents are with bedtime (sighs).

NDELLA: Okay, that is good to know. I mean, I love my bed, but I definitely do not want to go to bed at 3pm (she laughs). Okay, next season!

GEORGE: So, the season after Winter is Spring, but I want to talk about both Spring and Fall. They are a bit similar. Fall comes after Summer, which I will talk about soon.

NDELLA: Okay good.

GEORGE: In the Spring and Fall, it rains a lot. The weather is not too cold and too hot either. You must always carry an umbrella with you and wear rain boots when it rains if you want to. Did you know Fall is also called Autumn in some countries?

NDELLA: Yes, I knew that (rolls her eyes). C'mon, George, I read too, you know.

GEORGE: Okay, Okay, Okay, Miss 'know it all' (smirks and they both laugh).

Spring Autumn

GEORGE: Flowers blossom in Spring and leaves fall in the Fall (Autumn), whichever one you choose to call it. In these seasons, Spring and Fall, all you need to wear is a sweater to stay warm. Some people love this weather and do not even need warm clothes. Both are my favorite seasons. However, it is also allergy season in Spring for those who are allergic to pollens. My cousin is mostly allergic during this season and hates Spring because she is constantly sneezing, and her eyes are always itchy.

NDELLA: Oh gosh. Does she take any medication for that?

GEORGE: Yes, she does. There are other causes of allergies too such as pollens, insects, dairy, peanuts, sea food, et cetera.

NDELLA: Now I remember that one of my aunts is allergic to groundnuts. She recently found out.

GEORGE: Awwww. I really hate allergies. I wish we could all eat anything we wanted.

NDELLA: I wish so too.

GEORGE: Back to seasons. Do you have a favorite season?

NDELLA: George, I only have two options; I am not sure which one I like (they both laugh).

GEORGE: Summer! In the summer it gets so hot that you need to drink lots of water. It does not rain as much as in Spring and Fall, but when it does, you appreciate it as it cools down the air around you which is quite refreshing.

NDELLA: I wish it were like that here, especially when it is extremely hot.

GEORGE: People wear less clothing during the summer; they love to swim. It is fun during that season. Most people would rather play outside than be inside. I eat a lot of ice cream and popsicles during this season, and the sun comes out early and goes down as late as 9 pm. Because of

the long school break, I get to stay out late and have fun with friends and relatives. Some people take advantage of the summer and travel to other countries and have family time because their kids or nieces and nephews or grandkids are mostly on school break.

NDELLA: You are right about that. I love those days when the whole family gets to hang out and travel. I realized that not all kids my age can experience traveling. Some may never be able to travel to other countries in their lifetime. I hope that one day, when I am older, I can help other kids and their families experience this.

GEORGE: That is an excellent idea Ndella. I realize that some kids do not have that opportunity even here in my country.

NDELLA: No way! That is not true. That is a developed country.

GEORGE: The fact that it is a developed country does not necessarily mean everyone has the same opportunities. You will see when you come.

NDELLA: Wow! That sounds like another interesting conversation we are going to have.

GEORGE: Yeah! Well, that's all about that. Let us talk about the seasons in your country.

NDELLA: Mine is going to be short and brief, because we only have two seasons. The wet season and the dry season. The wet season is also called the rainy season; it is a season when there is heavy rainfall. However, there are times when the rain is rather light.

GEORGE: Oh wow! That means the farmers will not be able to harvest a lot when there is little or no rain.

NDELLA: Correct. However, during the heavy rains, they have a high increase of their farm produce. In this season, you will find puddles of water everywhere. Most children love to play in the rain. It is fun. In the wet season, water and air quality are great. The air outside is refreshing and the water is clean and cool.

LESS MARKET FOOD
FOOD PRICE INCREASE
10,000
LESS FARM PRODU

GEORGE: Ndella, when does the rain fall in your country?

NDELLA: Between May and September, and it's heavier in July and August.

GEORGE: And so, if the rain is less that year, that means fewer farm products, less food in the market, and an increase in prices of food?

NDELLA: Yuppp!

GEORGE: So how do people survive?

NDELLA: That is a good question. I have never thought about that. I will ask my parents when we are done.

GEORGE: I would like to know.

NDELLA: Me too. Let us get on to Dry Season. Dry season is that time of the year when there is little or no rain. This happens mostly in Africa, South America, and some parts of Asia. Arab countries also have harsh dry seasons. This is the reason some of these countries have deserts. Most of the time, the weather is dusty and some countries even experience dust storms. Little vegetation grows during dry seasons and some countries have long seasons of drought and lose their livestock and trees. However, trees and animals that reside near wells and rivers are more resistant to drought and survive.

NDELLA: In the dry season, there could be a shortage of farm produce due to the lack of water. Halfway through the dry season, farmers get ready by tilling the ground and planting seeds. They do this in anticipation of the Wet Season.

GLORY
BAPTIST
SCHOOL

GEORGE: It is funny how desert and dessert almost have the same spelling but different meanings.

NDELLA: You are right (they both laugh). An interesting thing occurs in some West African countries even though they may not have a desert. A cool and dry weather pattern known as the harmattan blows dusty winds from the Sahara Desert in North Africa over the whole of West Africa. It lasts from November to March. The harmattan weather in West Africa can be likened to the winter in the Western World. Though it may not be as cold as winter, it is still cold. So whenever we go out or go to school we have to wear sweaters to keep ourselves warm.

GEORGE: I have never heard of the harmattan winds either. I'd love to experience that.

NDELLA: Well, I cannot wait to experience yours either. There is also the 'New Yam Festival', which my friends in Ghana and Nigeria celebrate. I would like to attend one day. It is an annual cultural festival that is held at the end of the rainy season, I was told. It will be nice to experience that too.

GEORGE: Woaaahhhh, Ndella! That sounds exciting. I'm getting ideas now. We should plan that when you come.

NDELLA: (she laughs) Yes, we should. This was an amazing conversation. I learned a lot today.

GEORGE: Me too. I cannot wait to see you and your family. Next month, right?

NDELLA: Yupp, next month.

GEORGE: Have a good evening.

NDELLA: Have a good afternoon.

As Ndella and George ended their conversation, they both laughed with bright smiles and reflected on one word, SEASONS!

LESSONS FROM THE AUTHOR

Do you know that you, too, have life seasons? I don't mean Winter, Summer, Spring and Fall. I'm not referring to Dry or Wet Seasons either. These life seasons are experiences or changes that happen to you personally. There is a time when you are sad and a time when you are happy. A time when you fall sick and a time when you are healthy. There are times and seasons for everything in life. Good times and bad times, better days and worst days.

Your favorite season as a child can be when your parents get you an ice cream or a gift you wanted for Christmas or your Birthday. It can also be when you were given a treat at your favorite restaurant. Think about a vacation with your siblings or fun times at a family reunion. These are all good times you enjoy. It could be working hard towards getting into college or graduating with high honors and hope for the future. It could also be moving to a new school or a different country or making new friends.

Some seasons can be the opposite of being good. There are times when you feel hurt, disappointed or an illness or failure is staring at you. Sometimes you may feel betrayed or deserted. Nothing seems to work out well with you. There are times when you throw tantrums or get grounded, or your parents send you to the naughty corner. All these are seasons too.

Whether you are in a good season or bad season, never judge anyone. In life, people experience different seasons as they journey through the different phases of their lives. Seasons change. Do not judge the season someone is in if you have never experienced it. Even if you have experienced it, you may offer advice based on your experience, but do not force people to manage situations the way you did. People handle situations differently and the circumstances that led to your good or bad season may be different for someone else. Everyone has different capabilities.

Sometimes you enter seasons you never asked for or anticipated. This can be heartbreaking or frustrating. You may even wish you could have been more prepared. But think about this, sometimes you're never ready for rain or snow or for hot weather, but you still go out and build a snowman, or ice skate, or play in the rain, or go for a picnic. No matter what, do not let any season distract you from reaching your goals. You must keep going, stay focused, speak out, and seek help when you need it. Do your research and if you need to, take a break, but keep putting one foot in front of the other.

Note that each season does not last forever. We can never be fully prepared for any season. Whatever season you find yourself in, always prepare for the next. Save for rainy days, take your vitamins, do some workouts with your friends, take pictures, make memories, bake that cake you always wanted to, call that friend or family member on your mind right now, and drink lots of water. Every season is different, learn to manage each season differently.

THE END

ABOUT THE AUTHOR

JOIS DONKOR was born in Ghana, grew up in The Gambia, and currently resides in America. She earned her Master's Degree in Finance from the University of Wales in the United Kingdom and currently works as an Audit Consultant. Her pride and joy is working with children and youths for the past 20 years. This is one of the reasons why Jois started her nonprofit organization, Barrier Breakers Corner, where she encourages young people to step out on faith and defy the odds. Jois enjoys sharing people's stories of how they broke barriers through podcasting, youtubing, and supporting young people through various social events and media outlets. In her spare time, Author Jois Donkor enjoys reading and cooking for her family and friends. Her longtime dream of becoming a children's book author is being fulfilled through Seasons, which is the first of many other books to come.

Ingram Content Group UK Ltd.
Milton Keynes UK
UKHW050854040723
424525UK00003B/73

9 781088 092507